Library of Congress Cataloging-in-Publication Data

Bruce, Mandy.

    The Secret of the Ice Curtain / Mandy Bruce:
    illustrated by Jane Launchbury. -- 1st ed.
    p. cm. -- (The Adventures of the Sunset Patrol)
    Summary: The Sunset Patrol tries to locate the Shadowship's
    northern base in order to stop the killing of the whales.
ISBN: 0-8120-6096-2
    (1. Fantasy 2. Wildlife conservation - Fiction.
    3. Marine animals - Fiction) I. Launchbury, Jane, ill.
    II. Title. III. Series: Bruce, Mandy. Adventures of the
    Sunset Patrol.
PZ7.B8266Se 1988   88-14841
(E) - dc19   CIP
                                         AC

First edition for the United States published in 1988 by
Barron's Educational Series, Inc.

© Copyright 1988 by David Booth (Publishing) Ltd,
Designed and produced by David Booth (Publishing) Ltd,
8 Cranedown, Lewes, East Sussex BN7 3NA England.
All rights reserved.

All inquiries should be made to:
Barron's Educational Series, Inc.
250 Wireless Boulevard, Hauppauge, New York 11788

Library of Congress Catalog Card No. 88-14841
International Standard Book No. 0-8120-6096-2
Printed and manufactured in Italy.
890 987654321

The
Secret
of the
Ice Curtain

By Mandy Bruce
Illustrated by Jane Launchbury

Barron's
New York · Toronto

The day grew cold and darker but the Sunset ship sailed on, following Wishbone, the whale, through the waves.

They were racing to rescue the other whales who had been captured by the Shadowships. If they didn't get there quickly many of Wishbone's family would be killed.

"But we're the Sunset Patrol," whispered Red to his friend, Maple, "and we won't let that happen."

They huddled in their big coats and shivered as a cold breeze swept over Sunset's decks.

The Shadowships had taken the whales to their northern hideout.

It was a foggy bay, surrounded by a cold snowy land and guarded by the horrible one-eyed Icyclops.

Suddenly there was a terrible CRASH! and a cry of pain from Wishbone.

"Stop!" the whale shouted. "Stop! I swam straight into it!"

In front of them was a tall wall made of ice.

"An ice curtain!" cried Sunset. "I can't cut through this."

They followed the wall up and back again. It seemed to run for miles, and they couldn't find an opening.

An albatross flew by. The ship and the bird talked intently, then the albatross flew off.

The children looked worried, but Sunset explained.

The Shadowships' new defense was very clever. Not just one ice curtain but dozens—a whole maze of ice guarding the bay!

7

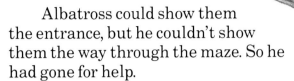

Albatross could show them the entrance, but he couldn't show them the way through the maze. So he had gone for help.

8

The bird was soon back. In his beak he carried a funny-looking fish which he dropped onto Sunset's deck with a loud, flabby plop. It was X-Ray the stingray, and he couldn't stop shivering and quivering.

"I w-w-wouldn't do this for j-j-just anyone, Sunset," said Ray. "I h-h-hate the c-c-cold."

The albatross led them to a secret gap in the curtain.

"Now, Ray," said Sunset. "Get to work."

The stingray plopped back into the water. His eyes grew bigger and bigger and redder and redder and lazer beams shot out from them.

The children were amazed! The stingray's super-powered X-ray eyes could see a route all the way through the maze!

10

The whale and the ship followed him along the creepy white corridors.

"Left a bit! Right a bit!" ordered the ray. "No, not up there, whale! It's a dead end."

Suddenly the ice curtains ended. They peered around the corner. They could see the snowy land and the bay.

And there were all the whales.

Along the shore the evil Icyclops were walking up and down carrying ice spears. Their bodies were white and spiky and each had one bright blue eye.

"Wishbone, go and join your family," said Sunset. "Tell them to be ready to leave when I sound my foghorn three times."

Wishbone nodded and, ever so quietly, he swam toward the other whales. Some of them recognized him but he went, "Ssshhh!"

14

"We must get out of here tonight,"
whispered one of Wishbone's friends. "The Shadowships
had gone upriver to be repaired, but they're coming
back soon. And then they're going to kill us!

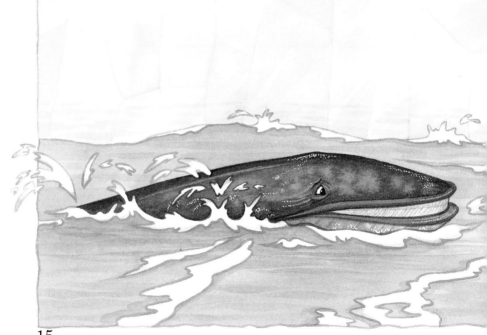

"We'd be dead anyway if it weren't for the children from the village. The Shadowships make them bring ice cream for the Icyclops every evening. And they've been smuggling in food for us as well."

Wishbone swam quickly back to the others. The great ship listened and then told them her plan. First Wishbone carried Red and Maple on his back to the shore. They jumped off and ran to find the village children.

Sunset and Wishbone waited.

At last they saw children coming over the hill toward the sea. They were carrying buckets of ice cream.

"Come and get it!" the children shouted to the Icyclops. As the creatures walked towards them Red called out, "OK! Ready—Aim—Fire!"

All together the children dipped their hands into their buckets and brought out snowballs made of ice cream which they hurled at the Icyclops.

"Aim for their eyes!" shouted Maple.

SPLAT! BOSH!

"Bull's eye!" shouted a little girl as some ice cream landed SPLODGE! right in an Icyclop's eye.

Ice cream was flying everywhere.

The Icyclops were running around and around but with ice cream in their eyes they couldn't see where they were going.

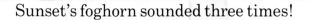

Sunset's foghorn sounded three times!

While the Icyclops were still confused, Red and
Maple ran to the water's edge and hopped on Wishbone's
back. They called the whales over to the ice curtains.

Then, with his X-ray eyes on full beam, Ray led
them one by one through the maze.

Sunset waited in the bay.

"Come on!" shouted the whales. But still Sunset waited. Then she heard what she had been waiting for—the rumble-dum of the Shadowships' engines.

As the two huge ships came into the bay they spotted Sunset and began firing their big guns.

Sunset turned and entered the maze. She put her engines on full power but traveled as slowly as possible. All the extra steam from her boilers she directed at the ice curtain.

At first there was a drip, then a drip-drip, then a drip-drip-drip. The heat of the steam was melting the horrible high walls.

Sunset steamed on and the Shadowships chased her deep into the maze.

The whales were safe in the open sea. They couldn't see Sunset but they could hear the Shadowships' guns.

BANG! BANG! BANG!

The shells which missed Sunset were hitting the ice curtains, now weak from all the steam. The outer wall of the maze began to crack.

Sunset sailed out of the maze and through the waves toward the whales. Behind her the maze shook as the Shadowships followed, still firing their guns.

BANG! CRACK! CRASH!

The whole maze collapsed—on top of the two Shadowships.

They couldn't follow now.

Everyone cheered.

Only Ray shivered miserably. By now he was quite blue with cold.

"Go and warm up in my boiler room and I'll give you a lift back to the south with Albatross," said Sunset. "You did a good job today, Ray."

"That's all r-r-right,"
said the Ray. "Only n-n-next
time I wish you'd make it a
w-w-warm war—and not a
cold one!"

30